D1100247

This LADYBIRD CLASSIC
belongs to

....

A History of Robin Hood

Long ago, in the time of the Normans
and the Saxons, there were very few
books. Most people could not read
and the tales they heard were sung
to them by travelling minstrels.

The hero of many of these stories was
Robin Hood. Some of the tales about
him appear in ancient manuscripts but,
over the years, the stories have been
changed and added to by many writers.

Chapter illustrations by Valeria Valenza

A catalogue record for this book is available from the British Library

Published by Ladybird Books Ltd
80 Strand London WC2R 0RL
A Penguin Company

001

© Ladybird Books Ltd MMXV

ISBN: 978-0-72329-559-4

Printed in China

LADYBIRD 🐞 CLASSICS

Robin Hood

Retold by Desmond Dunkerley
Illustrated by Laura Tolton

Contents

CHAPTER ONE

The Beggar Spy

THE FOREST CLEARING lay still
and quiet in the warm summer sunshine.
Nothing moved. It was as if all the wild
things there were holding their breath,
waiting for something to happen. Even
the leaves of the great oaks and beeches
of Sherwood Forest seemed barely to
rustle in the soft breeze.

Suddenly the figure of a small man ran

from the forest into the open. He paused for a moment to look back the way he had come. Then he raced across the clearing to the nearer of the two long grassy mounds which stood side by side at one end. He climbed quickly to the top and looked back once more before disappearing from sight as though into the ground itself.

Moments later the grass in the side of the other mound opened up like a trap door and the small man came out with a companion. The turf closed behind them and the two small figures looked quickly around them before darting off into the trees.

Life returned to the clearing. A wood pigeon settled on a branch and began its monotonous call. Two swallows dipped and wheeled low over the long grass in their search for insects and far off in the trees a cuckoo called.

But then came the sound of hooves. Sunlight flashed on arms and armour and the wood pigeon flew off with flapping wings as twelve horsemen rode into the glade.

CHAPTER TWO

The Squire and the Outlaws

THEIR LEADER WAS a young man dressed in chain mail. Although he carried a lance, his uncrested surcoat and shield showed that he was a knight's squire. A priest, a thin pale looking man, rode beside him. Ten men-at-arms sat patiently on their horses while their leaders talked.

'Now which way shall we go, Robert?' asked the priest anxiously. 'All these paths and trees look so alike, that I fear we shall never find the man we are looking for.' The squire laughed. 'If our lord is to be believed then we do not need to find him, for he will find us.'

'Then I wish he would do it quickly,' said the priest, looking anxiously around. 'I do not like this part of the forest.'

The squire signalled the little cavalcade forward again. Suddenly, a deep voice from the trees called, 'Stop! Do not move!' Robert raised his arm as men in green appeared on either side. 'We come in peace,' he said.

'With ten armed men?' asked the tall bowman who barred their way. 'How can that be?'

'The woods are full of desperate men, cut-throats and outlaws,' replied the young squire with a smile. 'It is important that the message this priest carries from my lord, Sir Richard of the Lee, is

delivered to the right person.'

'And who would that person be?' asked the bowman.

'You, if you are Robin Hood, as I suspect,' said Robert.

'You serve Sir Richard?' asked Robin.

'I am his squire, Robert of Stane Lea. My lord sends you greetings and this message.' The priest fumbled in a wallet at his belt and handed down a parchment scroll. Robin frowned as he read.

'Little John, we must bring our men to camp. Sir Richard sends news that everyone should hear.' He raised his horn and blew three short blasts followed by a longer one which echoed through the trees.

A dozen outlaws were already in the camp. More arrived until there were over sixty men in the clearing. When Robin saw that all but the scouts and sentries were there, he stood up.

'Lads,' he said in a loud, clear voice, 'our good friend Sir Richard of the Lee has sent me warning of a new plot which Guy of Gisborne and the Wrangby lords, together with the Sheriff of Nottingham, are hatching against us. Sir Richard sends it at great risk to himself. He heard it spoken of too loudly at the Shire Council.'

'A true friend,' said Friar Tuck. 'What is the warning, Robin?'

'They are to pay spies to wander through Sherwood disguised as beggars, pilgrims and poor travellers,' replied Robin. 'These are the kinds of people we usually only stop to help or feed. But now we must be on our guard against them, for they could be Gisborne's men searching for our hiding places.'

'So every traveller we meet, however harmless he may look, must be stopped and tested?' asked Little John.

'Yes, and tested well,' said Robin.

'If you find a Saxon who has been tempted by hunger to take the Sheriff's gold, point out to him the error of his ways and warn him away. If the spy is Norman, deal with him as you must.'

The outlaws went back to their work. Robin sent Will Scarlet to tell the scouts and sentries of the new danger. Then he took the squire and his men back to the path and set them on their way.

He watched until the horsemen were out of sight and then set off in the direction of his old home, Locksley Hall, to warn the villeins there not to talk to strangers about the food and clothes that the outlaws often sent them.

CHAPTER THREE

Robin Under Attack

ROBIN WALKED BENEATH the trees thinking of the new danger. He heard footsteps. Looking ahead, Robin saw a beggar coming towards him. He hid behind a tree and watched the man carefully. He wondered if this could be one of Gisborne's spies.

The stranger was very broad and carried a huge staff. He wore a patched cloak and an old wide-brimmed hat. Hanging from his shoulder was a bag of oatmeal such as all beggars carried. Tucked into his belt was a long knife in a leather sheath. Robin's suspicions were aroused, however, by the great leather boots which the man wore. They seemed of too good a quality for a beggar man.

'Stand fast!' called Robin. He stepped on to the track and reached for an arrow. The beggar swung round, the great staff whirled and the bow was knocked from Robin's hand. Surprised at the speed of the man's movements, Robin reached for his sword, but the staff whistled in another great sweep and the outlaw was knocked unconscious.

At that moment there came a shout from the trees. The beggar crouched over Robin, his hand on the hilt of his knife as if he were about to kill the outlaw. He looked up towards the sound with

a curse and ran off quickly.

Robin woke to find three anxious faces bending over him. Will Stutely helped him to sit up. 'Who did this to you, master?' he asked.

Robin smiled faintly. 'There was only one, Will,' he said. 'A sturdy man dressed as a beggar. I was not careful and he was too quick with his staff.'

The other two outlaws were young recruits who had only joined the band a short while ago.

They had been put in Will Stutely's care until they had learned the ways of the forest. 'Master,' said Ralph eagerly, 'let Michael and me go after the rogue and bring him back.'

Robin hesitated and looked at Will Stutely. Will nodded his head.

'Go carefully then, lads,' said Robin. He described the beggar to them and said, 'Do not be deceived by his looks. He is a

fierce man, and evil, too. I believe he may be the first of Gisborne's spies.'

The two young outlaws set off quickly through the trees. They had hardly taken up their positions when the beggar came stamping along.

'Hold, knave!' called Ralph and stepped out in front of him with drawn sword. Up came the staff, but the surprised beggar felt the weapon wrenched from his hands by Michael, who had leapt from the bushes behind him. Ralph dropped his sword and together the two young outlaws managed to wrestle the beggar to the ground. 'Now, rogue, you shall account to our master for the cowardly blow you struck him,' panted Ralph fiercely, kneeling on the man's chest.

The beggar's face took on a woeful expression. 'If your master is the tall forester I met a while back,' he whined, 'then I meant him no harm. I struck the

blow in fear for he startled me.'

'Tell that to Robin Hood,' said Michael without thinking.

'Was that really Robin Hood, the great outlaw, that I struck?' he groaned. 'He is the man I am looking for. I have something in my pouch here for him.' 'Show us then, beggar,' said Ralph.

The beggar knelt and fumbled in his bag. Suddenly the outlaws were blinded by a shower of oatmeal. As they staggered back, the beggar leapt to his feet. He seized his staff again and came swinging at them. The two outlaws ran. They knew that without their weapons they were no match for their opponent.

'Idiots we are,' panted Ralph.

'Aye,' agreed Michael. 'What will Robin and the others say?'

'All we have to show is this,' said Ralph. He opened the beggar's wallet and took out a parchment scroll.

CHAPTER FOUR

Richard Malbete

'THIS LETTER IS from Gisborne,' said Robin, looking at the scroll which Michael had given to him. He smoothed the parchment out and began to read.

'*To the worshipful High Sheriff of Nottingham, greetings. This is to introduce to you Richard Malbete. He is commended to us by my friend Sir Isenbart de Belame, Lord of Wrangby, for whom he has performed various* desperate tasks. He is a bold and cunning man and will lead the work for us of which we spoke. He knows of others to assist him and now needs the gold to pay them. Destroy this letter. Malbete is wanted by the King's Justices and there must be no proof that we have had dealings with him.'

There were angry murmurs from the outlaws as Robin finished reading. 'Malbete?' said Little John. 'What a strange sounding name. It's not one that I have heard.'

'It is Norman French,' said Friar Tuck. 'He seems to be well named for it means Evil Beast.'

'One we must be rid of,' said Robin sternly.

'Ralph and I could go and bring him to you,' said Michael eagerly. 'We have a score to settle and will not be tricked again.'

The outlaws laughed at Michael's

eagerness. They remembered how the two young outlaws had arrived covered in oatmeal.

'No, lads,' said Robin gently. 'It's more than that. I think if we can get rid of Malbete, now that we have this letter, their whole plan will crumble. But it will serve King Richard's cause and our own, if it is done lawfully. It is too dark to find him now. He is, by all accounts, a cunning as well as an evil rogue.'

'Perhaps he'll go back to Gisborne for another letter,' said Much.

'He would not dare,' said Robin. 'Then he would have to admit that the first letter had been taken from him. No, the Beast has gone to ground somewhere to make his plans, which gives us time to make ours.'

He thought for a moment and then with his hand to his mouth gave the gentle call of a roosting pigeon.

Almost immediately, a small man stepped silently from the shadows into the light of the fire. Michael and Ralph started back in alarm, but the outlaws who had been in Sherwood longer showed no surprise.

The little man stood before Robin, his dark eyes glittering in the light of the flames.

'Tull's heart is full of shame that he was not near when the Patched One struck you down,' he said.

'There is no place for shame in a heart as brave as yours, Little One,' said Robin. Tull lowered his head.

'Tell me,' Robin went on, 'is it known where this Patched One is now?'

'We followed him to the Abbey lodging house, and my brother Caw is watching him there,' replied Tull.

'St Mary's Abbey!' exclaimed Little John. 'Then he has turned away from Nottingham.'

'Perhaps he's going back to Gisborne after all,' said Stutely.

'More likely he has found a safe place to wait until he decides what to do. He knows that the Abbot is a friend of Gisborne's,' said Robin.

He turned to Tull, whose eyes had never left Robin's face. 'Tell me, Little One, has the Potter of Wentbridge entered Nottingham yet for the Fair?'

'No, master,' replied Tull. 'He is at the tavern just outside Nottingham. His horse took a stone in its hoof, which delayed him. He arrived after the curfew bell and threatened to break down the gate. He sits in the tavern now, drinking and cursing all Normans.'

The outlaws laughed at this for they knew the proud potter of old.

'Good,' said Robin joining in the laughter. 'Michael, Ralph; here is a chance to make amends for your foolishness. Go to the Mile Gate Tavern and tell the Wentbridge potter that Robin Hood begs a favour. I want to borrow his clothes, pots, his horse and cart and go to the Fair in his place.'

'Right, master,' said Michael. 'Come, Ralph!'

Little John laughed. 'Go carefully,' he said. 'This is no ordinary potter. He may teach you your second lesson of the day!'

'As he taught you, John, when you first met him,' said Much with a grin.

'Yes,' said Little John, and rubbed his head at the memory. 'I stopped the potter and asked him for his greenwood toll. The only toll I got was three blows from his staff. I can still feel them to this day!'

'Ask courteously, then,' Robin said to Michael. 'I have no doubt that he will come here with you. He has a true Saxon heart and, from what Tull says, his hatred of Normans is greater than ever at the moment.'

Michael and Ralph set off on their errand. Robin turned to Tull and said, 'Keep a close watch on St Mary's Abbey, Tull, and bring word to Little John if the Patched One moves from his bolt hole.'

The tiny forest man said nothing but placed his hand on his heart and was gone.

CHAPTER FIVE

Robin and the Potter

THE MARKET SQUARE at
Nottingham began to fill early. Traders
who lived in the town were already
setting up their stalls as the gates opened.
Then they were joined by the country
folk and travelling merchants, many of
whom had journeyed from far away.

One of the first to arrive was a large
fat potter with a red face, long straggly

hair and a bushy beard. He wore a floppy wide-brimmed hat and a big cloak. Whistling gaily, the potter drove his little cart straight to that part of the square where the steps of the castle came down into the market itself. Most traders avoided this particular spot for the steps led to the Sheriff's living quarters. He was a mean man and often came into the square to drive a bargain the traders dared not refuse.

No such fears seemed to worry the stout potter for he soon set up his stall right at the foot of the steps. He began loudly calling his wares above the din of the market place.

A crowd quickly gathered. His pots were good and the price he asked was so much less than they were worth that he soon had only a dozen pots left. Suddenly the great door above him opened and down the steps came Dame Margaret, the Sheriff's wife, with her serving girl. Attracted by the noise, she made for the crowd around the potter's stall. They parted respectfully to let her through. The potter swept off his cap and bowed low to her.

'Madam,' he said, 'a poor potter would be honoured if so fair a lady would accept, as a humble gift, these last twelve pots of mine.'

'Why, good master potter,' she said with a surprised but friendly smile, 'I thank you. These are fine and well-made pots, among the best I have seen.'

'Only the best would be good enough for you, my lady,' said the potter.

Dame Margaret smiled again. 'Next time I must pay you for your pots. You must be sure to let me know when you come to Nottingham again,' she said. 'Until then, may I repay you by asking you to eat with my lord Sheriff and me? The day's first meal is about to be served.'

So the potter found himself seated at the table next to the Sheriff and in company with twenty other guests or important members of the household. The meal had hardly begun when there was a great commotion at the door. The Sheriff, a thin, mean-looking man, glanced up from his plate to see the cause of the disturbance.

'Can I not eat in peace?' he called out irritably.

'A rough fellow is trying to force his way in, my lord,' replied a serving man who had run up. 'He says he must speak with you.'

The Sheriff pushed his meat away and speared an apple on his knife point. 'Must is not a word to use to me when I am eating. Throw the rogue out and whip him for his insolence,' he snarled.

There was more scuffling at the door as the guards obeyed the order.

'My lord Sheriff,' a harsh voice called loudly. 'I have a message for you from Sir Guy of Gisborne.'

'Hold!' called the Sheriff, thumping the table with his fist. 'Bring the rogue here. You have a message from Sir Guy, you say? Out with it then.'

'It was a written message, sir Sheriff,' said Richard Malbete. He shook off the two soldiers who held his arms.

'The letter, then, you fool, the letter?' snapped the Sheriff.

'My Lord, the letter was stolen from me as I came here through the forest,' replied Malbete. 'I was set upon by twenty men. Robin Hood's cut-throats most likely. If you would send to ...'

'Then you have no message after all,' the Sheriff interrupted angrily. 'What is more, you could be one of that band of

villains yourself, come here to spy on me.'
He turned to the guard. 'Whip the lying
knave and then see if a night in the stocks
will loosen his tongue.'

The beggar was dragged away and
talk at the table began again.

'I doubt this Robin Hood can be as
great a bowman as men say,' said a
merchant. 'No man alive could hit the
marks he is said to hit.'

'Saxon gossip!' said the captain of
the Castle Guard.

'They say he splits a stick at fifty
paces,' said the potter shyly.

'They say!' said the Norman. 'I say
– and I will wager on it – that I can come
as close to that as any Saxon. What say
you to that, potter?'

The potter glanced round the table.
'It seems, my lord Sheriff, that as I am
the only Saxon here, that challenge was
meant for me. But I am no longer of the

build to draw a bow,' he went on, patting his large stomach. 'Although I did so often enough in my youth, but if…'

The Norman captain gave a great shout of laughter. 'I didn't mean you, potter, though if you would care to live your youth again and take up the challenge, I'll let you shoot from the halfway mark.'

'Excellent!' cried the Sheriff, and standing up he led the way to the tilting yard. A stick was set in the ground and the Norman captain stepped back fifty paces. Drawing his short military bow back to full stretch he took careful aim. There was applause from the onlookers as the arrow thudded into the turf only two inches from the stick.

The captain looked pleased as he paced out the halfway mark and handed the bow to the potter.

'That was a fine shot,' said the potter.

Then he selected an arrow and took aim. There was an even greater shout as his arrow split the stick in two.

'By the saints,' cried the Sheriff, 'you are a better bowman than you are a trader, master potter.'

'It was a lucky shot,' said the potter modestly. 'I could not do it again.'

'I would like to know that for certain,' said the Norman captain ruefully.

So the potter took another arrow. He seemed to hesitate before he shot and the arrow missed the mark which pleased the Sheriff and the captain.

'I am more used to the Saxon longbow,' said the potter. 'That rogue you spoke of, Robin Hood, gave me one and…'

'You have met Robin Hood?' said the Sheriff suspiciously.

'Only passing through Sherwood Forest,' replied the potter. 'I shot a round with him then he gave me the bow

because I hit the mark a time or two.'

'Where in the forest was this?' asked the Sheriff eagerly. 'Do you know his hiding place? Could you lead me and my men there?'

The potter thought for a moment. 'He has his camp now in a place they call Witch Wood,' he said. He hesitated again. 'I could take you there, but the outlaw rogue would hear if too many of your men came too. Bring only a dozen or so.'

'See to it, captain,' agreed the Sheriff.

'One last thing,' said the potter. 'We must not leave before sunset. It would not do for me to be seen leading armed men into Sherwood. In the dusk, however, I might pass unrecognized.'

CHAPTER SIX

The Sheriff
is Tricked

THE POTTER LEFT the Sheriff and
mingled with the crowds in the market
place. He spent some time talking to
two small men, and by the direction of
their looks much of the conversation
concerned Richard Malbete, who sat in
the stocks red-faced and cursing angrily.

Just as the town gate was closing at
sunset a little cavalcade passed through.

The potter led the way, driving his cart. Then came the Sheriff with his Guard Captain, Hugo, followed by men-at-arms. The potter went deep into the forest, through glades and along narrow tracks.

'Are you sure you know the path, potter?' demanded the Sheriff.

'Robin Hood is nearby,' replied the potter. Suddenly the notes of a horn sounded and a huge man stepped out.

'Greetings, master potter,' he said cheerfully. 'Have you brought visitors?'

'Aye, Little John,' answered the potter. He jumped down from his cart and said, 'The Sheriff has come to visit us.'

Robin threw off the cloak and tunic.

'Robin Hood!' roared the Sheriff. 'You rogue!'

'No, sir Sheriff,' said Robin Hood, 'you are the rogue. That beggar, Malbete, whom you had whipped, did have a message from Gisborne as he said.

That letter was taken from him by two of my lads. It proves that you have employed a thief and a murderer, wanted for his crimes.'

The Sheriff spluttered with rage but Robin Hood went on sternly.

'I brought you here to give my men time to take Malbete from the stocks. They are now taking him, with your letter, to Sir Hubert de Warenne. He is loyal to King Richard and will see that he answers for his crimes. Go back to Nottingham, Sheriff. You will answer for your treachery to the King.'

The Sheriff's men dropped their weapons and the Sheriff led them off. The young captain was about to leave when suddenly he leant down from his horse.

'Was that a lucky shot, or did you miss the second time on purpose?' he asked.

Robin met his eyes. 'The miss was harder for me than the hit,' he said softly.

CHAPTER SEVEN

The Silver Arrow

'I SAY AGAIN it was a foolish thing to do, Gisborne,' said the Sheriff impatiently. 'Now de Warenne has your letter. He is King Richard's man and will hold it against us until the King returns.'

'If he ever does,' replied Sir Guy of Gisborne sullenly, 'and until then de Warenne can do nothing. But the Prince…'

'Prince John can do nothing about

your letter,' the Sheriff interrupted, 'and will not be pleased at your stupidity.'

The Norman knight stopped pacing. He thumped the table. 'You had Robin Hood here in this very castle, and let him go,' he raged.

'How was I to know that potter was Hood in disguise?' snapped the Sheriff.

'You should have known it when he split the stick,' snarled Gisborne. 'There is only one bowman in all England who can hit that mark.'

'The potter missed with his second shot,' said the Sheriff.

'On purpose, you fool, so that you would not know him,' raged the knight.

'This arguing will not get the letter back,' said the Sheriff, hoping to get the talk away from how he had been tricked.

Gisborne turned round angrily and said, 'Nothing will get the letter back, but if we could capture and hang

Robin Hood then Prince John would
at least think more kindly of us.'

'Agreed!' said the Sheriff. 'But how?'

'Your pardon, lords,' said a voice from
the shadows.

'Yes, Hugo, what is it?' demanded the
Sheriff.

'I watched the potter, Robin Hood
I mean, very carefully when he shot his
second arrow,' he said.

'Well what of that?' snarled Gisborne.

'He is probably the greatest bowman
in all of England. He is proud of his skill
and I know that it was hard for him to
miss deliberately. I do not think he could
miss again on purpose.'

'Come to the point, man,' said
Gisborne impatiently.

'The point, my lord, is that if you
announced a great archery contest to be
held here in Nottingham, Robin Hood
would be sure to enter. He would come in

disguise again, of course, but my men would be ready to arrest the winner.'

'Who would be Robin Hood!' said the Sheriff. 'It would never work,' he said doubtfully. 'He would not dare to come here again so soon.'

'I am sure he would,' said Hugo. 'To make doubly sure it could be a contest between Saxon and Norman. Hood is even prouder of his birth than he is of his skill with the bow.'

'What do you say, Gisborne?' asked the Sheriff.

'What have we to lose?' replied Gisborne. 'If we take a force of men-at-arms into the forest we are cut down by arrows from bowmen we often do not see. Belame's plan is useless now that his man, Malbete, has been taken. So let us try this way, to lure the wolf from his lair.'

• • •

'It's a trap, Robin,' said Little John urgently.

' Tell me again the words the Crier used, Will,' said Robin.

'We had delivered Malbete to the King's Justice,' said Scarlet. 'On our way back we lodged at Ashby for the night and as we left the next morning a crowd had gathered to hear the Crier. He said that an archery contest would take place in Nottingham a week from now to find whether a Saxon or a Norman would win the Silver Arrow prize and be champion archer of all England.'

'Everyone knows who is the greatest archer in England,' said Little John.

'It is not for the title or prize that I must enter,' said Robin quietly.

CHAPTER EIGHT

The Day of the Contest

WHEN THE DAY of the archery contest
arrived, there were many keen-eyed men
with suntanned faces among the crowd.
They carried bows and wore swords
beneath their long brown cloaks. They
had come in twos and threes as if they
came from different parts. Robin himself
was dressed in a tattered brown jerkin and
hood. He had let his hair and beard grow

longer than usual and his face was stained and dirty.

As there was no place large enough in the town itself, the contest was to take place on a great stretch of green below the walls. The keep of the castle loomed grey and menacing, and despite the gay flags and banners, it was towards the friendly trees of Sherwood – a mile away across open country – that Little John kept glancing anxiously.

He had noticed that many of the men-at-arms who surrounded the ground wore the livery of Gisborne.

Friar Tuck said, 'I fear that treachery is afoot.' They pushed their way through to the front of the crowd to be as close as possible to their leader.

Robin glanced at the raised platform on which the Sheriff sat with his wife and officers of his household. There was no sign of Gisborne, but Robin had also seen

the men-at-arms and knew that the knight would not be far away.

At a signal from the Sheriff, a trumpet sounded and the contest began. First came the shooting at an ordinary round target set two hundred yards away. Each of the eighty archers shot three arrows and any who did not place two shots within the inner ring did not shoot again. Then the target was placed at an even greater distance until only twenty bowmen were left.

This broad target was then removed and the narrow one set up. Ten failed in their first attempt at this and when it was moved back even further, all but four missed the mark. Diccon of Trent and the tall stranger were using the Saxon longbow, while Hugo and William Tirrel used the short military bow of the Normans.

Rivalry in the crowd now grew intense.

Diccon's name was chanted over and over again for he was well-liked by the Saxon villagers. There were shouts, too, for the tall stranger in the patched cloak. No one knew his name but he was a Saxon and had hit each mark first time. The Norman shouts were all for Hugo. Tirrel was one of Gisborne's grim-faced soldiers and disliked for his rough ways.

When the narrow target had been moved back as far as it would go and still not one of the four had missed, there was a delay while the marshals decided what new mark should be set up. Hugo and Tirrel waited silently while Diccon moved away to talk to friends in the crowd. Robin stood apart selecting the best arrow from the quiver at his back. They were all fine shafts, carefully made for the contest by Hal the Fletcher, who was new to the outlaw band.

As Robin tested an arrow for

straightness, a burly merchant walked out from the crowd. He put an arm around Robin's shoulders and said loudly, 'You are a fine bowman, friend, for all your rough appearance.'

Robin looked up from under his hood and recognized the man as one that he had once helped. The merchant looked keenly at the outlaw and then spoke again in a quiet and urgent whisper. 'If you are the one I think you are, be careful! Gisborne is just inside the town gate with twenty mounted men ready to cut off your escape when you make for Sherwood across the open land.'

Robin nodded his thanks and the man stepped back into the crowd, saying loudly again for all to hear, 'Brush the hair from your eyes, beggar man, and shoot straight. You are a Saxon, remember!'

The marshals finished their discussions and announced the next target. There were shouts and cries of amazement from the crowd when they heard that a stick was to be placed fifty yards away. To make the task even more difficult, the bowmen were to stand with their backs to the target, turn when commanded and shoot before the count of three. Such a shot left almost no time for careful aiming and needed the hand and eye of a true master bowman.

'Are you happy about this test of your skill?' The Chief Marshal asked each of the four men in turn.

'If I hit the mark it will be more by luck than by any skill of mine,' said the honest Saxon, Diccon of Trent, 'but I will try.'

'It's an impossible shot, but so be it,' snarled Gisborne's man, Tirrel.

Captain Hugo and the tall beggar each looked at each other then nodded their agreement. Straws were drawn to decide the order of shooting. The crowd grew quiet as Diccon stood first with his back to the target. 'Turn – one – two – three!' called the marshal. Diccon shot and the crowd let out a great shout as if they themselves could encourage the arrow itself to its mark. The shout turned to a groan as the arrow buried itself in the turf a hand's span from the stick.

'It was a good shot,' said Hugo sportingly as he took his place. The roar that followed his arrow rose to a shout of wonder as the shaft thumped into the ground at the base of the mark. Tirrel missed by a full yard and as the tall, untidy figure of the last contestant stepped to the line the crowd were already acclaiming Hugo the winner. No one thought that the Norman captain's shot could be bettered. Their shouts turned to cries of absolute amazement as Robin turned and shot without even waiting for the count of three.

'A split!' they cried. 'He has split the stick! The beggar wins!'

'As I said it would be – a lucky shot!' snarled Tirrel. Diccon ran to Robin and seized his hand. 'No, a master's shot!' he cried. Hugo, too, shook Robin's hand but gazed at him as he did so.

'It was one or the other,' he said. 'Could you do it a second time and prove which?'

Robin met the other's gaze and remembered their last meeting. Then without a word he took another arrow and turned his back to the wand. Again he shot instantly without waiting for the count or to aim.

'He has split his first arrow!' a voice called in amazement, and a huge roar of approval rose from the crowd.

'My question stands answered,' said Hugo looking at Robin with admiration in his eyes. 'Now, master bowman, you

must be presented with your prize,' and taking Robin's arm he led him to the space in front of the Sheriff.

Here the outlaw leader stood in the open and alone. A fanfare of trumpets sounded and the Sheriff rose to his feet. Then as well as the Silver Arrow, he held in his hand a parchment, which he unrolled.

'*In the name of His Royal Highness, Prince John, Regent of all England, I arrest thee, Robin Hood, outlaw, for...*'

The rest of the words were lost in the shouting. A trumpet blared and the Sheriff's soldiers tried to join Gisborne's men, but the crowd pressed so hard upon them that they were unable to do so.

Pushing Hugo away, Robin Hood threw off his brown cloak and stood there proudly in Lincoln green. His horn rang out above the noise and the outlaws, also in green now, ran towards the sound.

Little John, Friar Tuck, Scarlet and

Much were first at Robin's side.

'Swords, lads,' shouted Robin and they cut through a gap in the crowd. 'Make for Sherwood!' he called and the outlaws retreated, turning now and again to send a flight of arrows at their pursuers.

Suddenly Little John fell with a groan, a Norman arrow in his leg. 'Leave me,' he gasped. 'Leave me here, for the horsemen are coming. Look!' Robin saw Gisborne's cavalry coming across the field, but he stooped to hoist Little John on to his back. A hand held him back. 'I'll get the big fellow to the trees while you keep off the horseman,' said Diccon of Trent.

'You are outside the law with us,' Robin warned quickly.

'So be it,' said Diccon.

Robin formed his men into a solid rank, as Diccon stumbled off with Little John. Then, at his command, a flight of arrows hummed into the galloping

Normans, bringing down horses and riders and throwing all into confusion. One man rode on into the trees, but fell almost at once. Tull dropped from a branch and retrieved a black arrow from the dead man's throat before giving the terrifying shriek of a wild cat.

'On, you fools, after them!' raged Gisborne, urging his confused riders. But none dared to face the darkness or that fierce cat's cry.

'By Saint Denis,' cried the knight, 'are you Norman soldiers or are you...' There was a sudden droning noise and the Norman's horse reared. With a groan Gisborne pitched from the saddle, an arrow jutting from his visor.

'That last was your best shot of the day,' said Diccon of Trent, as he followed his new leader deep into Sherwood Forest.

'Aye,' agreed Robin Hood, 'to rid the world of such an evil man was worth the Sheriff's Silver Arrow.'

Collect more fantastic
LADYBIRD CLASSICS

9781409311232

9781409311256

9781409311287

9781409311249

9781409311270

9781409311263

9781409312215

9781409312222

9781409313557

9781409313564

9781409313571

9781409313588

9780723270874

9780723270867

9780723295600